Tiny Timothy Turtle

For Kristie
who sometimes feels like Timothy

For a free color catalog describing Gareth Stevens' list of high-quality children's books, call 1-800-341-3569 (USA) or 1-800-461-9120 (Canada).

Library of Congress Cataloging-in-Publication Data

Leditschke, Anna.
    Tiny Timothy Turtle / by Anna Leditschke; illustrated by Carol
McLean-Carr. — North American ed.
      p. cm.
    Summary: A young turtle, smaller than the other animals he associates
with, finds there are some advantages to being small.
    ISBN 0-8368-0667-0
    1. Turtles—Fiction. [1. Marine animals—Fiction. 2. Size—Fiction.
3. Stories in rhyme.] I. McLean-Carr, Carol, ill. II. Title.
PZ8.3.L498Ti   1991   [E]—dc20   91-2020

North American edition first published in 1991 by
Gareth Stevens Children's Books
1555 North RiverCenter Drive, Suite 201
Milwaukee, Wisconsin 53212, USA

U.S. edition copyright © 1991. First published in Australia in 1989 by William Collins
Pty. Ltd., with an original text copyright © 1989 by Anna Leditschke. Illustrations
copyright © 1989 by Carol McLean-Carr.

Printed in the United States of America

1 2 3 4 5 6 7 8 9 95 94 93 92 91

Tiny Timothy Turtle

by Anna Leditschke

Illustrated by Carol McLean-Carr

Gareth Stevens Children's Books

MILWAUKEE

Tiny Timothy Turtle says,
"Sometimes it's hard to be so small.

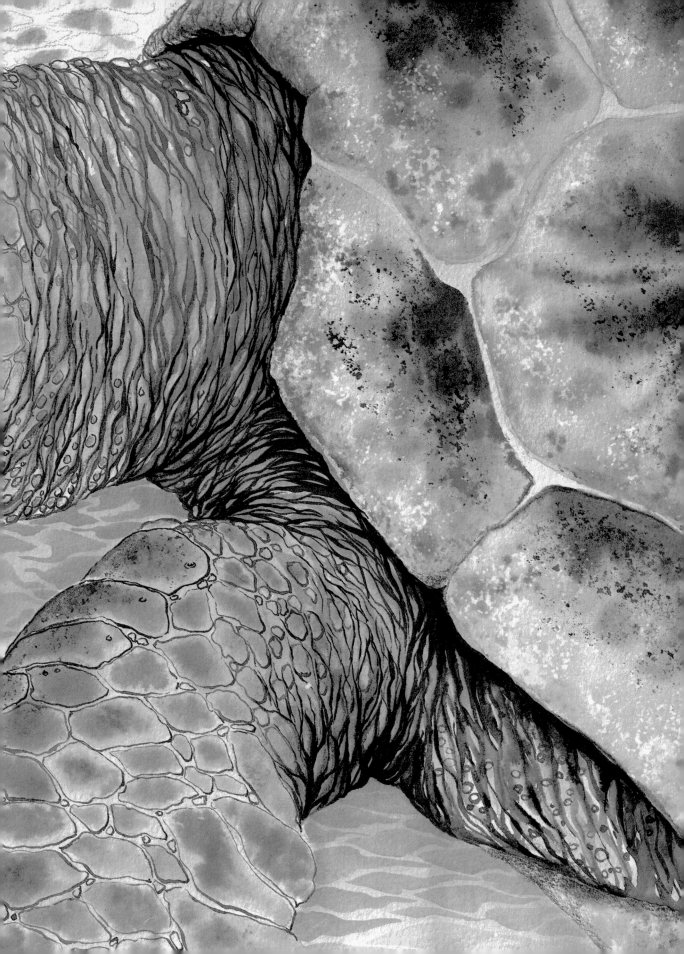

Everything else seems so very tall.

Everyone calls me a runt or a pest,
just 'cause I'm smaller
than all of the rest.

I swim and I swim with all of my might,

but I'm never as fast . . .

. . . well, not quite."

Tiny Timothy Turtle says,
"My mom and dad, they say I'll grow . . .

. . . but it may take a year or so.

But being small *can* help, you see.

No one gets past the sharks . . .

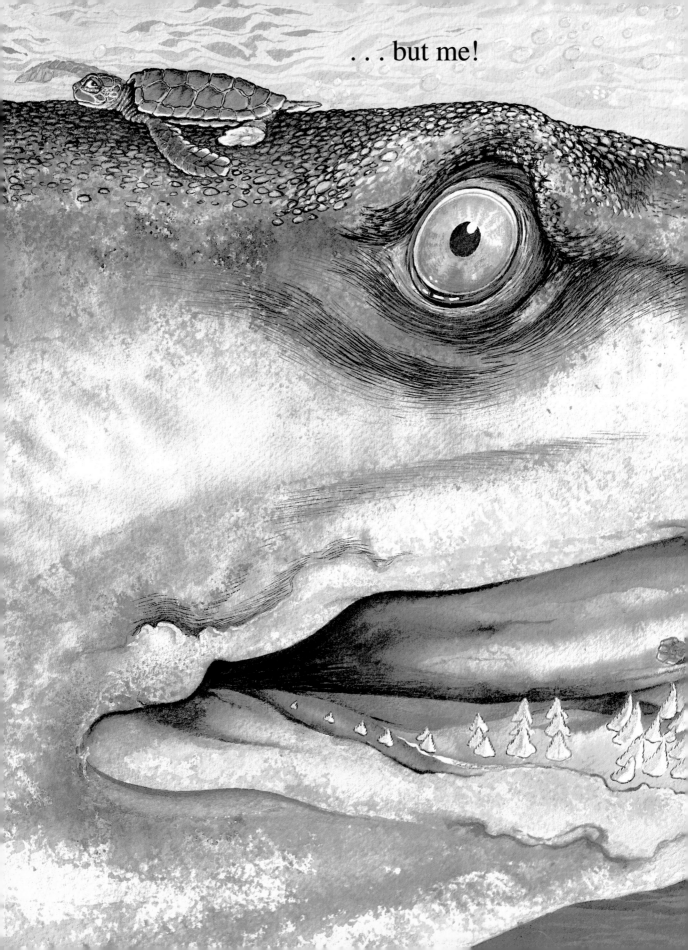

. . . but me!

My mom and dad, they said I'd grow,

and I did . . . in a year or so!"

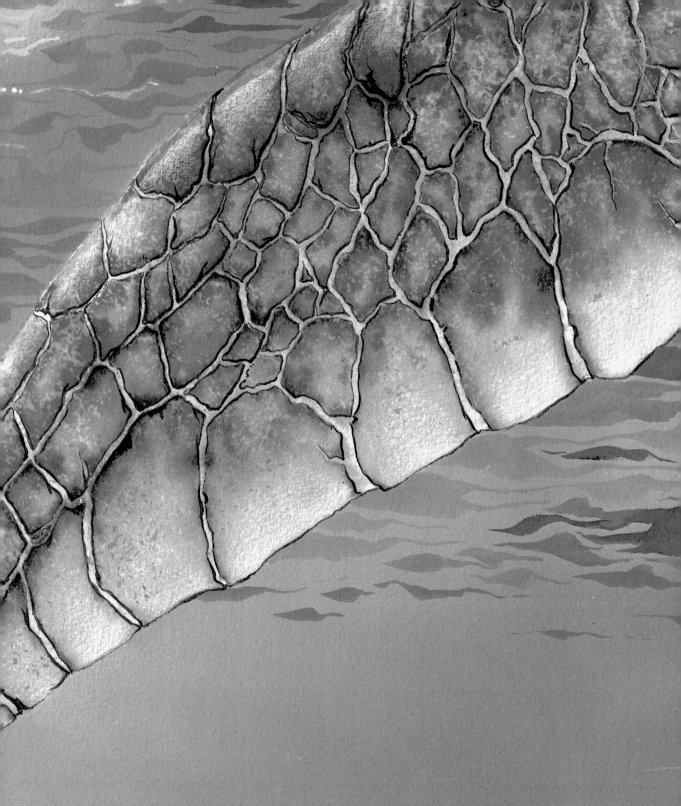

"Now no one dares to call me a pest . . .